# An Evening at Alfie's

*Also by Shirley Hughes*

ALFIE'S FEET
ALFIE GETS IN FIRST
ALFIE GIVES A HAND

*For Dorothy Edwards*

Library of Congress Cataloging in Publication Data. Hughes, Shirley. An evening at Alfie's. Summary: A burst pipe causes chaos over the upstairs landing while Alfie's parents are out, but Alfie, his baby-sitter, and her parents finally find a solution. 1. Children's stories, English. [1. Family life—Fiction. 2. Baby sitters—Fiction. 3. England—Fiction] I. Title.   PZ7.H87395Ev  1985   [E]    84-11297
ISBN 0-688-04122-1     ISBN 0-688-04123-X (lib. bdg.)

# An Evening at Alfie's

## Shirley Hughes

Lothrop, Lee & Shepard Books
New York

One cold, winter evening . . .

Alfie and his little sister, Annie Rose, were
ready for bed,

Mom and Dad were ready to go out,

and the MacNallys' daughter, Maureen, was in the living room. She had come to look after Alfie and Annie Rose while Mom and Dad went to a party.

Alfie and Maureen waved goodbye from the window.

Annie Rose was already in her crib. Soon she settled down and went to sleep.

Alfie liked Maureen. She always read him a story
when she came to baby-sit.

Tonight Alfie wanted the story about Noah and
his ark full of animals. Alfie liked to hear how
the rain came drip, drip, drip, and then
splash! splash! splash! and then rushing
everywhere, until the whole world was
covered with water.

When Maureen had finished the story it was
time for Alfie to go to bed. She came upstairs to
tuck him in. They had to be very quiet and talk
in whispers so they wouldn't wake up Annie Rose.

Maureen gave Alfie a good-night hug and went
downstairs, leaving the door a little bit open.

Alfie didn't feel sleepy. He lay in bed
looking at the patch of light on the ceiling. For
a long time all was quiet. Then he heard a funny
noise outside in the hall.

Alfie sat up. The noise was just outside his door. Drip, drip, drip! Soon it got quicker. It changed to drip-drip, drip-drip, drip-drip! It was getting louder too.

Alfie got out of bed and peeped around the door. There was a puddle on the floor. He looked up. Water was splashing into the puddle from the ceiling, drip-drip, drip-drip, drip-drip! It was raining inside the house!

Alfie went downstairs. Maureen was doing her homework in front of the television.

"It's raining upstairs," Alfie told her.

Alfie and Maureen went up to look. The puddle was getting bigger. The drip-drip, drip-drip, drip-drip had turned into a splash! splash! splash!

"Hmm, looks like a burst pipe," said Maureen. A plumber was one of the things she wanted to be when she left school.

"Better get a bucket," she said. So Alfie showed her where the bucket was kept, in the kitchen cupboard with the brushes and brooms.

But now the water was dripping down in another place. Alfie and Maureen found two of Mom's big mixing bowls and put them underneath the drips.

Maureen got on the telephone to her mother. The MacNallys lived just across the street. Mrs. MacNally was there in a moment.

"Oh dear, oh dear, it's ruining your mother's floor!" cried Mrs. MacNally. "Fetch some towels, Maureen!"

Just then Annie Rose woke up and began to cry.
"Shh, shh, there, there," said Mrs. MacNally,
bending over her crib. But Annie Rose only looked
at her and cried louder.

Mrs. MacNally ran back out to Maureen and Alfie. Now the drips were coming from lots of different places, splash, splash, splash!

"We ought to turn the water off at the main," said Maureen, "but I don't know how you do it. I think I'd better fetch Dad."

While she was gone, Mrs. MacNally mopped
and mopped, and emptied brimming bowls, and in
between mopping and emptying she ran to try to
comfort Annie Rose. But Annie Rose went on
crying and crying. The drips came faster and faster.

Now there were a lot of puddles on the floor. Alfie paddled in them for a while. It was fun, but the water was very cold. He thought that soon perhaps the whole street would be covered with water, and they would all have to float away in a boat, like Noah's ark.

Soon Maureen came running
upstairs with Mr. MacNally,
wearing his bedroom slippers,
close behind her.

"What's all this, then?" said
Mr. MacNally, looking at all the
water pouring down.

He put his head around the
bedroom door. He and Annie
Rose were old friends.

"Dear, dear, what's all this?"
he said in a very kind voice.

Then he went downstairs
and found a valve under the
stairs and turned it off, just
like that.

"So *that's* where it is," said
Maureen.

Soon the water stopped pouring down through the ceiling, splash! splash! splash! and became a drip-drip, drip-drip, drip-drip, and then a

drip . . . drip . . . . . . drip . . . . . . . . drip . . . . . . . . . . .
and then it stopped altogether.

"Oh, thank goodness for that!" said Mrs. MacNally.

"I'll know how to do it next time," said Maureen.

But Annie Rose was still crying.

Alfie went into the bedroom to see if he could cheer her up. Tears were rolling down her cheeks and soaking into her blanket.

"Don't cry, Annie Rose," said Alfie. He put his hand through the bars of her crib and patted her very gently, as he had seen Mom do sometimes.

Annie Rose still wore diapers at night.

"Annie Rose is wet," Alfie told everyone. "And her bed's wet too. I expect that's why she's crying."

"Why, so she is, poor little mite!" said Mrs. MacNally.

When Annie Rose was dry and comfortable again, Mrs. MacNally put her on the living-room sofa with Alfie, and tucked a quilt around them. Then she gave them each a cookie.

Annie Rose was quite cheerful now. She got very friendly with Mr. MacNally and he let her play a game with him, taking off his glasses and putting them on again. Then she sucked her thumb and leaned up against Alfie, and Alfie leaned up against her. When Mom and Dad came home, they were both fast asleep.

Next morning Mom told Alfie not to turn on the taps until the plumber had come to fix the burst pipe.

Alfie didn't mind not having to wash. He'd had enough water the evening before to last for a long time.